OUT OF THE WILD

A SHORT STORY COLLECTION

FRANCESCA MCMAHON

Edited by
CARLY CATT

CONTENTS

The Into The Wild Series   v
Wolf-to-Human Language   vii
Content Warnings   ix

ECHOES OF THE PAST

Chapter 1   3
Chapter 2   9
Chapter 3   13
Chapter 4   17
Chapter 5   21
Epilogue   27

BEFORE I GO

Chapter 1   31
Chapter 2   37
Chapter 3   41
Chapter 4   47
Chapter 5   51
Epilogue   57

FINDING HOME

Chapter 1   65
Chapter 2   71
Chapter 3   75
Chapter 4   81
Chapter 5   87
Chapter 6   93
Epilogue   101

Also by Francesca McMahon   107
Acknowledgments   109
About the Author   111

Cover Illustration by Ranpakoka
Cover Typography by MiblArt
Interior Design by AB Books
Editing by Carly Catt

ISBN: 978-1-918113-05-1 (Ebook edition)
ISBN: 978-1-918113-06-8 (Paperback edition)

WOLF-TO-HUMAN LANGUAGE

- Den – Home
- False Forest – A Town
- False Sun – A light
- False wolves - dogs
- Suns/Moons – Days
- Moon cycle – One month
- Mother Wolf – "God"/Mother Nature/Spirit
- Night lights - Stars
- Savage Blood – Rabies
- Season – One year
- Shadows pass – Hours
- Smoking sticks – Guns
- Span's distance – A Mile
- Stolen sunrise – Fire pit
- Sun pass – One day
- Sun's fall - Sunset

- Sun's fever – Fire
- Sun's time – Summer
- The cold season – Winter months
- White Coat - Doctor

CONTENT WARNINGS

This work contains depictions of child abuse, gore, racism, animal death, animal cruelty, and depression.

ECHOES
OF THE
PAST

FRANCESCA MCMAHON

CHAPTER 1

*E*cho didn't regret much. He'd not lived enough to have regrets that haunted him – until now that was.

He thought when he left his pack at the start of the hunting season, he wouldn't have to struggle to find food. He'd been one of the strongest runners of the pack. It should have been simple enough. Unfortunately for him, he hadn't fully considered the fact that now, as a lone wolf, he had no territory of his own that he could hunt in without facing retaliation.

Stories of the lone wolf were often spoken in packs with a level of awe that would make any youngling excited for the day they struck off alone to find their own home. Just like most stories, it seemed, the elders of his pack had left out some very important details.

Licking his most recent wound, a bite to his back leg, Echo recuperated by the mountainside. It wasn't the most comfortable location – the cliff-face having collapsed multiple times, leaving sharp gravel dotted across the ground, and the nearest woods abandoned, barring the few bird nests in the high trees, too high for Echo to reach and steal an egg or two from.

The only benefit of the mountainside was that no pack ruled this land. Here he could rest comfortably without worrying he'd be set upon by a rival wolf. Adding to that was the fact that, with the shadows of the woods and the mountain, his black fur allowed him to blend in. For now, he'd be able to keep himself out of sight. Echo was good at that.

It was part of why he left his first pack, the one he was born into. He had always been the quiet one, easily able to fade into the background. Though it made him an expert hunter, his prey falling into his trap before they even realised what was happening, it didn't help him socialise and work with the family as well as they expected him to.

Echo enjoyed being the silent support, but his pack had not appreciated his skill set. So, he struck out on his own to find one that would. Now though, after being without a pack for nearly a whole moon cycle, he was beginning to realise how difficult finding a new home was. Moreover, without a pack, he'd been struggling to hunt. He'd been without food now longer than he'd been without his family.

As if to remind him, his stomach twinged, making him wince. Echo had gone without meals before when the cold seasons were at their peak, but this was just too much. He wasn't sure how much longer he could go.

Should I risk trespassing in Nikita's territory? Echo thought, staring out into the distance, searching for the fallen tree to mark the border of their land. It wasn't hard to spot. Nikita's territory was a force to be reckoned with. With a Den made of a fallen tree protected by a grove of tightly grown trees and sharp-edged bushes, it was no wonder it was a prime location for pup rearing and hunting deer and caribou. *Would it be worth straying into the outskirts of their land?*

Then he remembered Nikita's youngest, a white-as-the-moon, furred she-wolf who'd helped chase him the first time he travelled into their territory by accident while with his old pack.

Maybe not, he decided, *no reason to get on the wrong end of that wolf's teeth.*

Echo sighed and lowered his head to his paws. It would be a waste to put himself at risk for a meal he may not even get. He would just have to find another part of the Forest to hunt in, and maybe, if he was lucky, he'd find a pack that would take him in soon after.

It was just as he was about to rest that he heard it.

The heartbeat of a predator.

A fox, to be exact.

Echo opened his eyes and sought the enemy. Wolves and foxes were born rivals. And though Echo was starving, he had enough energy in him to kill the red-furred demon if needed.

What surprised Echo was that instead of seeing the fox in the main valley with him, he watched as the creature slipped out from within the trees between the two mountains ahead of him. But that wasn't the only thing that caught Echo's attention.

No, what drew his eye and his nose was the scent of a fresh kill. Being dragged out from the trees by the fox was a small, limp carcass, and from the look of its bloodied body, it was ready to be feasted upon. Echo stood and, blending into the surrounding shadows, quietly stalked towards the kill. He'd never seen a creature like that before.

Even at a distance, he could make out the strange, tight, curled fur of the black-headed creature, though most of it was now matted with blood. The beast was small, smaller than the fox, in fact. Echo wondered if maybe it was the young of whatever creature it was born from.

Echo was close enough now to see the beads of the fox's yellow eyes as they locked onto him in the shadows.

This is mine, wolf! the fox snarled, stepping in front of its meal.

She would have looked ferocious and brave if her pounding heart didn't give away the fear she was feeling. Foxes weren't ones for confrontation; they were scavengers at heart. Thankfully for her, Echo wasn't either. But she didn't need to know that.

Smiling to show off his teeth, Echo stepped forward. **I believe you are mistaken, fox.** He stepped closer still, thanking his luck as his rival stepped backwards, preparing to run. **You are giving me this...creature.**

Jumping forward, Echo snapped his jaws at the fox who, as he expected, yelped in panic and turned tail and ran into the protection of the bushes.

Echo held back a sigh of relief, just in case the fox was still in ears' reach, and turned to the kill. Before he could even question what it was, his stomach clenched in desperate pain, and Echo dove in to eat.

The prey was like nothing he'd ever tasted. As the blood and muscle slipped down his throat and coated his maw, Echo tried to place a comparison but found none. Caribou was fattier in its taste, while deer was stringy and flavoursome. But this? It was tough yet smooth when pulled apart. The white, curly fur sticking to his teeth as he tore off muscle. The blood that dribbled down Echo's throat was warm and intense in its flavour. Echo couldn't stop himself from tearing more and more pieces of meat from the beast's flesh, savouring every bite of it.

Where in the Forest did this creature come from?

It was only after Echo had eaten his fill that he remembered where the fox had come from. Turning to his right, he stared into the empty grove of trees where no creature lived or slept.

Then, in the distance, just barely visible, Echo saw a light. It wasn't the light of the moon or the sun. No, this light felt...wrong somehow. Yet, it proved one important thing to Echo.

There was a world beyond the Forest.

A land ripe for hunting.

CHAPTER 2

$\mathcal{E}$cho didn't go straight away. He wasn't stupid enough to explore an unknown world without scouting it first. This wasn't his first hunting trip. To start, he kept to the shadows of the trees, examining the land from a distance.

After only a short while of watching, he could tell that this was a strange place indeed. Close to him, Echo could make out the white curly furred beasts he had eaten. They were surrounded by a protective shield circling around them. That confused Echo until he saw the oddly shaped Dens that, irregularly, had figures entering and leaving them. Looking at the shield around his prey, Echo could only assume that the white furred animals belonged to whomever ruled this foreign land.

For three suns, Echo watched and tracked the movements of these figures. He noticed that his prey were left alone in this shielded space. They were only visited by the figures once a day, if that. Once, one of the white beasts was taken by their masters. It was never returned after that, though Echo couldn't tell what they did on those visits.

On the night of the fourth sun, using the cover of darkness to his advantage, Echo made his move into the land. He could only be caught if these strange creatures had eyesight as good as him and spotted his golden eyes in the night. And from how often he'd seen them walk into one another, he doubted they did.

He took his time, airing on the side of caution above anything else. He was on his own in this land. There was no point taking unnecessary risks when there was no one to help him.

Making a wide arc around the shield, he caught a glimpse of something shining on the shield. Coming closer, he spotted a line of silver with sharpened points and knew to be wary. They reminded him of the prickle branches from the Forest, and he had always been told to avoid those. So he did.

Staying close to the cage, Echo watched the white curled beasts as they ate the grass at their feet, barely aware of his presence. He searched the barrier for any openings that he could use to his advantage, but found none that could accommodate for his size.

It was as he came closer to the strange Dens of the larger beings that lived in them that Echo's nose twitched.

Turning away from his target, he looked towards the land in front of him. Random snowless paths had been dug between the Dens, a guide leading to each individual one.

Lowering his nose to the dirt path, Echo sought the smell that had gained his attention. It was late enough that the beings here were nowhere in sight, but Echo kept to the shadows anyway.

Whatever they had killed was fresh. And with none of the locals in sight, the meal was free for the taking.

Around the corner of one of the strange Dens, Echo found it. A freshly stripped carcass of what he assumed to be one of the white curled creatures. It was left hanging from a strange branch attached to the Den.

Echo looked around, anxiety making his fur stand on end.

Is this too easy? he thought, his heartbeat picking up at the idea. But for the first time, he didn't listen to his instincts.

Stepping forward, Echo reached out for the meat. His teeth were just brushing the bloodied flesh when the Den's entrance was thrown wide open, engulfing him in light, almost blinding him in its intensity.

There, standing in front of him, with a stick in hand, was one of the beings he had only seen from a distance. Now, seeing them up close, Echo realised the mistake he had made. Here, standing in front of him, was the monster from the stories he had been told about as a pup.

He hadn't found just any land.

This was the land of the humans.

CHAPTER 3

*A*wolf never freezes. It goes against their very instinct to do so. To freeze means to die. Yet, here Echo was. Frozen in place. His eyes locked with the icy blue of the humans in front of him.

Echo had never seen a human before. He'd only been told stories of them when he was a pup. They were so different from how he'd pictured them. Their faces were flat, only a short nose stuck out from it, which only made Echo wonder how they had survived as long as they had. They were tall though, towering over him with ease, and from how long their legs were, Echo found himself no longer wondering how humans had survived for so long. Instead, he was surprised that the wolves of the Forest had survived with these beings as their neighbours.

Echo had never felt fear like this before.

That was until the human took a deep breath before letting out a bellowing shout, not at Echo, but to the world around them.

It is calling for its pack.

He'd never figured out how many humans lived here during his scouting, so he didn't know how many would come. All he knew was he didn't want to find out the hard way.

So, just like the fox he had cornered a time ago, he turned and ran.

Ran faster than he'd ever had to before.

BANG.

Something hit the ground next to him hard, kicking up rocks and dirt from the power of it. It took every part of Echo to fight against his instincts to turn and find what that noise was.

He kept running.

BANG.

Almost reaching the barrier where the human's prey lived, Echo could hear their strange guttural groans of terror as they ran around in circles in their prison. They couldn't escape. And that would be to Echo's advantage.

Echo charged straight for them.

They would not attack their own food source, he thought hopefully.

With a run up, and adrenaline in his blood, Echo leaped over the barrier with relative ease, though he landed awkwardly on the uneven ground on the other side. The prey became more distressed, running this way and that.

Echo was thankful, and ran straight for the centre of them, hoping to use the beasts as a shield from the humans.

BANG.

One of the white curled creatures fell with a thump to his left. Echo only just had enough time to turn and see the bloodied mess of the beast to realise that that bang wasn't just to scare.

It was to kill.

Panic seized him. He'd seen nothing like this before and found himself too afraid to stop the fear from taking over. While he knew he should have zig-zagged between the beasts, all he could do was run straight to the barrier, praying his speed was enough to get him to safety.

You will make it, he grunted to himself as he leapt as high as he could into the air, high enough to clear the barricade.

BANG.

A high-pitched yelp echoed into the air, loud enough that Echo was sure all the wolves of the Forest could hear it.

Echo found himself on the ground on the other side of the prickle fence, but still on the ground, too stunned to move. When he tried to stand, he whimpered as he put weight on his right back leg.

He had been the one to cry out in pain.

Turning to his side, he saw a large gash at the top of his leg, right where the joint moved for running. But right now, he was in no condition to do so. In the distance behind him, he heard the growing shouts of the humans. Echo, pulling his focus away from the pain as much as he could, counted each individual voice he could hear.

Six...no, eight humans.

When he got to twelve, he stopped counting. One was terrifying enough. He didn't need to know how many it would take to bring an end to his life.

Echo tried to stand again, biting back a whimper as the pain shot through him again. He'd felt nothing like this before. No bite or scratch from a fellow animal had ever hurt this badly. It didn't look deep like most other injuries he had sustained, but each step he attempted to make tore through his leg like he was being hit with the human's bang again and again.

He dropped to the ground and rolled to his side. The snow was cold around him, which was strange. He'd never really felt the cold before. Most wolves didn't.

With his injured leg flaring with heat, Echo attempted to rub his leg into the snow to cool it. But it only seemed to make the pain worse.

The human's voices were getting closer.

Echo sighed and dropped his head to the ground. He was going to die here. Alone. And no wolf would ever know.

Then he heard it.

A howl in the distance, just beyond the mountains. It was the words within the howl that caught his attention the most.

Make it home.

CHAPTER 4

*D*o **not give up**, the wolf cried, the sound reverberating across the expanse of the open land all the way to Echo's injured side.

He didn't know who was calling to him. It was a voice he'd never heard before. At that moment, though, it didn't matter who it was. All that mattered was that there was someone out there fighting for him.

Someone wants me to survive.

Well, who was he to deny them?

Echo pushed himself up to his feet, clenching his jaw to hold back the cry of pain. The wound was splitting open wider, and from his time on the ground, the surrounding snow and mud had irritated the inflamed area more. It would not be easy making it to the safety of the Forest.

BANG.

The solid barrier directly behind him splintered from the shot and the ground at his back legs sprayed snow.

Running was going to hurt, but better to hurt than be dead.

Echo had been injured before. All creatures had. It was impossible to avoid that in this world. This was just the first time that Echo was wounded while actively attempting to escape a predator.

As he pushed forward, his damaged leg moved awkwardly, always a second out of time from his other legs' movements, making his run as clumsy as a freshly born pup's. Even as he could feel the wound tearing more across his flank, he kept pushing himself.

His ears twitched at the sound of the approaching humans. Thankfully this time, he had enough sense to adapt his movements, zig-zagging across the open land as best he could, changing direction when necessary. Keeping an easily recognisable pattern would do no good.

It was when Echo was around ten strides away from the mountains and the grove that something heavy came crashing into his back, knocking him down.

Trying to get back up, desperate to escape, he struggled more. The projectile had hit him right on the flank, catching the side of the wound and making it throb violently.

The humans weren't far now, and it was they who had hit him just right to render him useless. Again.

Echo turned in the direction in which they would come, hoping that at least whatever they planned would be quick.

As their small heads peeked over the hill's horizon, Echo took a breath. Ready to face them down to the end. What he didn't expect was, as the humans' faces became visible, so did the body of a pure white, furred she-wolf that soared over the top of Echo, charging towards the humans in a fierce frenzy.

Her first victim was the figure with the stick in their hands. She got to them before they could even raise it and ran right through their legs, before turning around and running into the legs of the companion next to them, knocking them into one another. With two on the ground in a heap together and the stick dropped to the ground, the wolf got down to work with the others, keeping them away from the stick. She may not have seen what it did, but it wasn't hard to deduce the significance it had to the humans.

The white wolf didn't attack the humans; that'd just be asking for retaliation that the Forest didn't need. But from the looks of it, she knew just the right way to confuse and disorientate them.

Distracted by his rescuer, Echo missed the first time she called out to him.

Move, you fool! she snapped, her beautiful golden eyes snapping to his, if only briefly, before she continued to distract the humans. This time by stealing the stick from them.

This time, she didn't have to say it again.

Pushing himself up to his feet, Echo limped towards the trees. He didn't stop to turn and see what had happened to the white wolf, too concerned that he wouldn't make it, even with her help.

It seemed that didn't matter in the end when the blurring figure of the she-wolf shot past him, barking out to **Run faster!** as she went.

Only then did he turn and found the befuddled humans regrouping after being terrorised by the wolf. Echo would not stick around for that. Though his leg protested, Echo pushed himself hard, following the path of the white wolf into the protection of the Forest.

They could only hope that the enemy wouldn't follow.

CHAPTER 5

They ran and ran, putting as much distance between them and the other world as possible, only stopping when Echo's injury forced him to rest.

Collapsing to the ground, Echo took multiple deep breaths, exhaustion sinking into his bones. He was only just aware of the surrounding land – his head so woozy that he wasn't sure what was real and what was a dream.

Is it common for you to have a death wish?

That brought Echo to consciousness. He'd forgotten the she-wolf was still there. Lifting his head from the ground, he turned towards the voice and finally took in his rescuer. When he did, he almost forgot to breathe.

Larka? he said, surprise in his voice.

The white wolf frowned, clearly taken aback at how Echo knew her, though he wasn't sure why. Most wolves knew of Larka. The fearsome daughter of Nikita, the very wolf who'd chased him away a season ago. Larka was well-known for being aggressive with trespassers. Her mother had been guiding her to become the new matriarch of their pack. All the same, she wasn't the sort of wolf you forgot.

What kind of fool enters human land? Larka asked, pacing back and forth.

I did not know it was–

Even worse! You entered their land ignorant of what to expect and found yourself trapped by the first measly obstacle placed in front of you.

Echo's star-struck feeling evaporated in an instant.

I would not exactly call losing the ability of my leg a measly obstacle! How about you be hit with this human's bang stick and see how you react? he snarled, attempting to jump to his feet to face her, but they buckled beneath him before he'd even made it to all four. *Not exactly the show of strength I was hoping for*, Echo thought bitterly.

You do not need to see how I would react. I would not be stupid enough to cross into human territory, Larka retorted, turning her nose up at him as she walked past.

A growl grew in Echo's throat. He was tired, hungry, and injured. He didn't need to put up with this wolf.

Then why did you come to my rescue, oh mighty wolf? he snapped.

Larka rounded on him, but just as she was about to snap out a retort, she paused, confused. It was here, Echo realised, that she didn't even know why she had come to his rescue.

Thankfully for her, Larka seemed to be the wolf who could work her way out of any situation.

Because...you would not have made it out alone. I was doing you a favour. Now I am owed one in return.

This time, Echo thought it best not to argue back. He'd learnt the hard way many times how a she-wolf deals with those who insult them. And Larka seemed to have even less patience than his sisters.

As an awkward silence fell over the two of them, Echo took the time to study Larka staring off into the distance. He'd not been this close to her before, seeing as the last time featured him running away instead of talking. It was surprising to see her in a different light. A kinder one.

Her piercing gold eyes searched the surrounding land, alert just as a leader would be. She stood tall and proud above him, showing off her strength as she held her head high. Her snowy white fur, once pristine, was now matted with mud and dirt from her rescue, but that only made her more beautiful.

Does it hurt? Larka asked quietly, breaking their silence.

She was looking at his swollen and bloody hind leg, frowning in frustration. *Or was that worry?* he thought as he studied her closely.

Before Echo could even answer, Larka was stepping forward towards his injured leg. Most wolves would have attacked her. They weren't from the same pack. They had no reason to trust the other. Yet, Echo did. And Larka trusted him to not attack.

A warm tongue ran across the wound on his leg. Echo flopped his head to the ground to stop himself from crying out at the pounding in his leg. Larka kept going. Starting first with the bloodied tear itself, pushing hard enough to hurt, she cleaned the wound itself and the cuts surrounding it. After a while, the pain faded to a dull throbbing, and after two shadows had passed, it dwindled to a bearable ache.

Without even having to speak, Larka helped Echo to his feet. Though it hurt to put pressure on his back leg, it wasn't as bad as before. To his surprise, Larka stayed close to his side as he stretched out the leg with a gentle walk in a circle. When he could walk comfortably enough, he turned to thank her. It was only as their eyes locked that he found himself unable to do so.

You are welcome, Larka said with a smile, as if she had heard his thoughts.

Echo barked a laugh in response. He couldn't believe how quickly their interactions had changed from where they began to now. Unfortunately for him, Larka noticed this as well. And already Echo could tell how prideful she was.

Stepping back from him, Larka turned away. **I will head home now. Do not get yourself killed while I am gone.**

You intend to come back? Echo asked, curious. Though from the sharp look that was sent his way, clearly that wasn't what Larka wanted to hear. So, he came at it from another angle.

I am truly grateful, Larka, he said, lowering himself to her to show the genuineness of his words. **I know you risked much to help me. If there is anything I can offer in service, I will provide it.**

Echo, with his head still low, raised his eyes towards Larka for her reaction. He could catch a small smile on her lips before she hid it away.

My mother can never know of this. Do you understand me?

Stepping forward, ignoring the bite in his leg from his wound, Echo's eyes held Larka's. They stood in a comfortable silence as they watched one another. It was as if time had frozen as they stood there.

Never know about what? he asked, a charming lilt to his words as he felt his heart race quietly. **We have only just met.**

Without another word, Larka turned and sped away. Echo watched her until he could no longer see her in the distance.

Later that night, after finding somewhere safe to rest and heal, Echo replayed their meeting over in his mind. As he fell asleep to the thoughts of the future, he hoped it wouldn't be long until he saw Larka again.

EPILOGUE

$\mathcal{A}$ season had passed since Echo's adventure into the world of the humans that almost cost him his life but gave him one instead. Without that reckless venture, he never would have met Larka, his soul.

It didn't take long after her rescue for the two to find themselves unable to be without one another. Being apart was painful. Such was the case with most soulmates. So, they made it so they wouldn't be.

She brought Echo into Nikita's pack one moon cycle after the two had found each other. Another moon passed, and by then, Nikita had passed the mantle of leadership onto the two of them.

Now, with pups of their own to care for, Echo and Larka were thriving in their lands. Not much had changed in how the pack was run with their leadership. There was only one thing that sparked a change to the dynamics of the Forest.

After witnessing first hand the power of the humans, Echo recommended expanding their territory to the edge of the mountain treeline. In doing so, they could guarantee that no wolf or other being would cross the lands into their enemy's territory again.

They patrolled the border at the turn of each season, marking their territory and monitoring the predators in that area of the Forest. Their message spread far and wide: this land is not to be crossed, or suffer the consequences.

With Larka and Echo settled and raising their young, they found themselves at peace. Soon all memories of the humans faded into just that, memories. Their fear, buried but still there, dimmed with it.

It wouldn't be until three seasons later that these memories returned when they found a human child abandoned in their lands.

But that is a story for another day.

BEFORE I GO

FRANCESCA MCMAHON

CHAPTER 1

*J*amie had never been interrogated before, but she was pretty sure that these people had no idea what they were doing. For one, they couldn't seem to figure out who was the bad cop and who was the good one.

"Now, honey," the red-haired woman said, crouching next to the seat they'd put Jamie in. Jamie tried not to roll her eyes at the word "honey". "You know it'll be better for you if you tell us. We're just trying to help you out."

This time Jamie let her eyes roll. She knew a trap if ever she heard one. Adults always said that before they'd tell her off. That became all the more clear as she watched the woman stand sharply, angry now.

"Tell us how you found out about the girl."

At least she knew why they'd brought her here. Not that that would make a difference. She wasn't going to say a word to them. She would keep her promise.

"Where's my dad?" Jamie asked, trying not to smile. "I'm only ten, he should be here with me, right?"

The balding blond man that, until then, had been sitting stoically in the corner, stood up at that and strode over. He was a lot taller than Jamie expected, though most adults were.

"He's given us permission to talk to you. Now answer Dr Cora's question. How did you find out about that dangerous wild girl?"

Jamie bit her tongue to stop herself. She wanted to tell these awful people that Artemis wasn't dangerous. Artemis wasn't even wild. She was a wolf, just like her family in the forest, and she'd gone back to where she belonged. But Jamie couldn't say that. She couldn't show how connected to Artemis she was. No, she had to separate herself as much as possible.

"I didn't, Miss." Jamie turned to Cora, trying not to let venom coat her words. She knew what this woman had done. "I just met her that night and thought we were playing, then she hurt me." Raising her hand to show them her slowly scarring palm. "See."

Cora hmm'd at her answer, as she sat herself up on the table, cold blue eyes never leaving Jamie's oak-coloured ones.

"Yet, didn't she attack Mrs Hammond because of you?" she asked, head tilted. "In fact, I remember having to stitch up and give Mrs Hammond a tetanus shot because that wild child bit her over nothing."

Jamie clenched her hands into fists and buried them in her lap. Unfortunately, Cora's fox-like eyes caught the movement instantly, and she smiled. Of course she'd see what Mrs Hammond did to her as nothing. Bullying a child for not belonging was perfectly acceptable here. The whole town had done it ever since her father had dropped her off with her great aunt.

Jamie took a calming breath through her nose before answering.

"I saw her that night, yeah." She leant back against the chair in an attempt to look bored. "But I didn't even realise it was the same girl from that night outside your lab."

The blond, balding man began pacing at that.

"You didn't know it was the same girl?"

Shrugging, Jamie shook her head. "No. I only saw her at night." She rubbed her left eye with one of her hands. "I guess a lot of people here look the same."

"Really? That's what you're going with?" the bald man asked, incredulous.

Jamie frowned, feigning confusion.

"Now, Dick," Cora started, stopping only to glare at Jamie giggling at her words. "Richard, it is a somewhat reasonable answer."

Dick turned to Jamie, eyes narrowed. "Why did you go with her to the sheep's pen if you didn't know her then, huh?"

Her eyes went watery at that and she looked away from them, trying to calm herself down. At least this answer would be closer to the truth than the others.

"None of the other kids play with me." Jamie turned back to the adults in the room, quickly brushing away any sign of tears. "She would." Then Jamie remembered her role. "Or at least, I thought she would until..." She raised her injured hand.

"And you never saw her between these two instances?"

Jamie shook her head.

"You never came into the lab to see her?"

She shook her head again.

"So if we brought her back, you wouldn't want to see her?"

"Why would I?" Jamie questioned.

"Well, little Artemis, that's what I called her by the way." Cora smiled, though there wasn't much genuineness to it. "She seemed to take a fancy to you. I caught her watching you from her room's window once. I'm sure it would have been nice to have a friend here. It must be hard being alone, Jamie."

"Why would I want to be friends with that..." Jamie stuttered. "...that ... half-breed? Did you not see what she did?" She raised her scarred palm again. "I want nothing to do with her."

Cora raised her hands in surrender, though Jamie could see the smile on her face. Seemed it wasn't just one child she enjoyed torturing.

"That's enough."

The three people in the room turned towards the now open door. Standing there was Jamie's father, William Gander-Yoon. He was wearing his usual attire: a comfortable and well-fitted jumper that he would tuck into his workers slacks. His bright blue eyes, so different from Jamie's, were hard as stone as he glared at the two adults in the room.

"I believe she's answered your questions as best a *child* can," William snapped, his folded arms tensed enough to show just how much stronger he was than those here. "You've had Jamie here to talk for an hour now. That'll do."

"Now, Mr Gander, I'm sure—" Dick started, but was cut off by a raised hand by Jamie's dad.

"It's Gander-Yoon. And seeing as neither of you are a member of law enforcement and are interrogating a child about another child who, as you well know, was held here illegally for research, I think we're done." He pulled out his satellite phone which he always kept with him. "Unless you would like me to contact the real authorities."

Dick stepped back, his own hands raised.

"No need to be hasty, Mr Gander … Yoon," Cora said. The throbbing vein in her neck caught Jamie's attention, making her squirm. "We were finishing anyway."

Turning back to her, Cora lowered herself to Jamie's side, her blue eyes piercing hers till the hair on the back of Jamie's neck stood up.

"Thank you for your help, Jamie, you've been most insightful."

Cora smiled with all teeth, and for a moment, Jamie pictured Cora attacking her with those very pearly whites. With that look of pure evil in her eyes, she wondered if Cora was picturing the same thing.

Getting up from her chair, without another word, she rushed to her dad's side and took his outstretched hand.

As the two of them quickly left Cora's laboratory building and headed for their current home, Jamie only had one thing on her mind.

Would they really go after Artemis again?

CHAPTER 2

*B*eing ten was the worst thing she could be right now.

Artemis was in danger of being hunted down and captured again, and there was nothing that Jamie, a tiny ten-year-old girl, could do to stop them. Not that she wasn't searching for a way to do it all by herself. She may be young, but she knew how to work the system.

First things first, tricking her father into—

"What do you need?"

Bugger, she thought as her dad's all-knowing eyes landed on hers with a smile.

"I don't need anything..." Jamie started, unconvincingly stepping away from her dad's armchair, properly chastised. "I was just wondering, uhm, when's your next trip?"

Her dad turned her then, eyebrow raised, disbelieving. Thankfully for her, he played along for the meantime.

"If things work out all right here, I'll be travelling again by winter's end. So a month from now, I'd say." He nodded his head in agreement to himself as if approving his own words before he turned back to Jamie with a smile. "What would you like me to bring back this time?"

Jamie didn't have an answer to that. She was still trying to process what he had said. A month from now? He'd not even been back that long since his previous adventure. How could he leave so soon after that? Especially after everything she had told and shown him. Even more so, after he'd seen what Dr Cora and Dick were like.

His smile fell at her face, seemingly recognising the change in her mood. He closed the book he had been reading and put it aside. Climbing out of the chair, he patted the cushion for her, which Jamie took obediently. Her dad sat on the floor, looking up at her.

After she'd told her story about Artemis in this chair, whenever she had something to share, her dad would have her sit in the armchair and he'd watch her from the ground. It made her feel grown up in a way – which she definitely needed right now.

"How can you leave after what they said?" Jamie asked, her high-pitched voice masking the level of anger she felt towards him. She'd grown used to him abandoning her for his adventures, but she wouldn't allow it when it came to Artemis. She deserved to be protected more than anything. "I thought you cared about the wolves."

William frowned at that. "What makes you think I don't anymore?" It wasn't a patronising statement, in fact it was one of pure curiosity.

"Artemis is a wolf..." Jamie started, thinking for a moment that she may sound childish saying that. She knew that Artemis was, obviously, a human. But she didn't belong with humans, that much was clear. "So that means you're abandoning a wolf to be hunted. Right?"

Jamie watched her dad nod his head in agreement, and for

a second, she wondered if what he had taught her about his love of nature was all a lie. He came from this village after all. The people here were cruel in their very nature, hateful of anything that wasn't like them. Which, as Jamie realised when she arrived, included her as much as it did Artemis. She'd always looked like her mum, Yoon Seon-mi, more than her father. That was a problem here.

Could her father be the same? Could he be just as unforgiving of someone's differences like the people he grew up with were?

A hand touched her knee, drawing her attention back to her dad. Jamie saw his kind and patient smile directed at her. It seemed he knew what she was thinking.

"I would never abandon the wild," he said, his voice firm and direct. "There is just nothing that I myself can do here."

Jamie deflated at that, her head dropping back into the armchair cushion. She could hardly believe that he was giving up this easily. What happened to the man who climbed the tallest mountain to the peak even after everyone told him he was crazy? Or the man who stood up to the bullies in that interrogation room? Jamie felt disappointment rise in her chest.

"However," he continued, his fingers poking at her knee to make her laugh, "there may be someone I can call that could help us. But it's risky."

"Why?" Jamie asked, leaning forward, pushing his hand away in mild annoyance.

His smile fell slightly but returned quickly enough that Jamie didn't think much of it.

"Artemis is a rare case of a feral—" William stopped, changing his mind on what he wanted to say. "Of a wolf-child. Most humans can't survive long in the environment Artemis grew up in, let alone alongside a pack of wild animals. It's an incredibly rare phenomenon. Something many scientists, even myself, would be fascinated to explore."

Jamie nodded along, though she didn't really understand much of what he was saying.

"The problem is…" He rubbed his hand over his beard in thought. "If I contact the people I need to for help and they can't, it'd be like sending up a flare for Artemis' position. It could put her at more risk of being captured."

Jamie didn't like the sound of that.

She'd worked far too hard to help Artemis escape back home for it to be undone by her attempts to protect her. What were the things adults said? She's between a rock and a fireplace? Adults made no sense.

"It's up to you, Jamie," her dad said, patting her knee. "You know Artemis better than me. You'll know what's best for her. Let me know what you want me to do and I'll do it."

Her dad stood up then, his knees cracking as he did. He seemed more tired than usual. Jamie didn't realise she was frowning in worry until her dad laid a coarse hand against her cheek.

"Don't worry, it's just a sign that I should probably retire from being in the field soon," he said with a cheeky smile. "That'll just mean more time for hot chocolate with you."

Jamie smiled. And as easily as that, her decision was made.

"Call them."

CHAPTER 3

ora had done something. That much was obvious.
Materia had never exactly been thrilled to have
Jamie here, but when her dad had returned, they'd been a
little more forthcoming. However, something had changed
since her interrogation with Cora.

Now, wherever Jamie's dad and she went, the gossip-filled
mouths followed. They'd not even been able to buy their
usual portion of lamb meat from the butcher; the old man
holding a blood-stained knife in his hand ordered them to
leave his shop. In the end, they'd had to travel out to the
nearest city, about an hour's drive away, to collect their
needed supplies for the next few weeks.

Her dad wouldn't let her go out alone anymore. He didn't
say why, but she knew he was worried. She could sense it in
his jittery hands as they walked through the streets one
afternoon.

A woman bumped into Jamie, not hard, but enough to
make her tumble into her dad's side. Jamie was too stunned
to say a thing.

"What a disrespectful child," the woman said tersely. When Jamie looked up at her, surprised, she found the woman curling up her lip in disgust and brushing non-existent dirt from her clothing where she'd knocked into Jamie. "She got it from her mother, you know. Such a shame her father didn't teach her better."

Scowling after the woman, Jamie went to step forward, ready to fight, when her dad's hand landed on her shoulder.

"Let's head to the house, Jamie-bear," he said quietly, using the pet name her mum had used all the time when she was young to keep her calm. Raising his voice, he continued, "The old bat wouldn't know respect if it hit her in the face."

The woman turned her head back to them in shock, only to receive the darkest glare Jamie had ever seen from her dad. The cruel woman stormed off after that.

"Come on, we'll take a walk further away from town next time. You don't deserve this."

"Why?" was all Jamie could say as her dad pushed his hand against her back, rushing them as fast as her legs could go back to the house.

"Materia always had an issue with people who didn't follow their status quo." They walked past the lab then, and though they walked past quickly, it wasn't hard to spot Dr Cora watching them. "I have a feeling that the news of your interrogation has been put out there."

As they entered the house, kicking off their shoes, her dad looked out the door's window, worried.

"They seem to know you were holding something back, though God knows how they do. That Cora has always been —" He stepped away from the door and sighed. "No, all the people here have always been too cruel. That's why I left all those years ago."

Jamie frowned at that.

"Why'd you bring me here?"

William closed his eyes and rubbed a hand down his face.

"Because I hoped maybe they'd changed."

He walked away then, heading upstairs towards his room. Jamie was tempted to follow him, but something about the wistful sadness in his voice made her decide against it. Usually when he was like this, it meant that he was missing her mum. She understood. Jamie liked being alone with her memories of her too.

Jamie had only been seven when her mum, Seon-mi, had died, but in those seven years she was the best mum out there.

She travelled a lot like dad but never for too long. It was she who'd started the tradition of telling adventure stories of their expeditions. She'd also been the one who'd passed on the love of wolves to Jamie.

The strongest memory she had of her mum was when she was six. Jamie had been sitting on her lap, her head tucked into her mum's neck. She remembered, even now, the smell of blossoms that always came from her. Her beautifully long, dark hair had been pulled back and away from her face, allowing Jamie to look up and see her smile from where she sat. Her mum had the best smile. It could make you feel at home the moment you saw it.

That day she told the story of a family of wolves. A family that, against all predictions from the scientists, persevered in their large numbers through the worst snow storm since records began. They'd all been convinced that, with how bad it had been, not only would the new-born pups have died, many of the pack may have as well.

Then, when the storm cleared and their team went in search of the wolves, they found them in a nearby cave. Every single one of them was there. From the matriarch and her mate to the youngest pup who'd grown larger during the storm.

"It should have been impossible," Jamie could hear her saying. "Yet, there they were. Stronger than ever. That's when I knew."

"Knew what?" Jamie had asked, curious.

Her mum had turned to her, her brown eyes holding Jamie's, her smile widening, showing off her teeth, perfect in their imperfect crookedness.

"That wolves are the superior family unit," she'd said with a laugh, leaning forward to rub her nose back and forth over Jamie's. "That's why our family's a pack, right?"

Jamie had just laughed and laughed.

As she sat now by the fireplace, she reached out for her toy cat she'd left on the table by her dad's book. It was a great comfort when memories of her mum overwhelmed her.

She wasn't exactly sad anymore. It had been three years since it had happened. But there was an emptiness there still. One that Jamie had almost forgotten existed when she'd met Artemis.

Artemis had made her feel whole again somehow.

The time they'd spent together in the lab, as brief as it usually had to be, were the best times of Jamie's life. She'd not had anyone around to talk to much since her mum had gone. Barely had anyone wanting to listen to her talk except for the few times her dad would come back from his trips.

Jamie had talked way more than she had in a long time when she was with Artemis. Even though Artemis couldn't understand a word she said, Jamie never felt that she was not being listened to.

Artemis would sit there in silence, watching her, smiling, nodding her head for her to continue if she stopped. She was just as happy being around Jamie as Jamie was being around her. Or at least, that's what it looked like.

Squeezing the soft belly of the cat toy, Jamie stared into its glassy eyes.

"Do you think she's safe?"

No answer.

"I hope she got home okay."

No answer.

"You don't think Dr Cora will go after her again, do you?"

No answer.

"How long do you think Artemis was kept here for?"

No answer.

"Will Artemis remember me?"

She didn't have time to wait for the lack of answer before she heard the clamouring of feet down the staircase. When her dad burst through the door, Jamie jumped, surprised at the roughness in his actions.

"They called back," he said, his blue eyes alight in excitement and his smile wider than Jamie had seen it in a long time. "Jamie, the people who could help save Artemis called back."

Jamie dropped the cat toy.

"I have to go meet them," he continued, practically thrumming in excitement. "They're about a day's drive from here, but I have to go to present evidence for Artemis' case."

Jamie's heart sank.

"You have to go?" she whispered, reaching for her toy again.

Her dad heard the change in her tone instantly, and the excitement faded from his body. Coming to her side, he knelt down in front of her.

"Only for a few days, Jamie-bear." He smiled, his hand resting on her shoulder. "It could be our one chance to get the protection Artemis and her pack deserve. The chance to make sure these people go nowhere near Swen Forest again."

Jamie stayed quiet.

"Do you trust me?"

Looking up into his sincere blue eyes, Jamie held back a sigh. The fact is, she didn't. He'd made too many promises in the past, both to her and mum, that he never kept. How could she trust him with this?

"Yes." Lie.

He smiled wider, thrilled.

"I won't be gone long. I promise."

His bags were already packed. Turned out he'd never unpacked them. Within the hour, he was in the car, pulling away from the house and leaving the town and Jamie behind. It reminded her too much of the first time, almost a year ago, when he'd dumped her here.

As his car faded in the distance, Jamie turned to go back into the house when a strange flickering light caught her in the eye. She looked to see what it was, and the blood drained from her face the moment she laid eyes on it.

On a pair of quad bikes, three men with hunting guns were preparing their bags for a journey. They were dressed in white fleeces lined with arctic fox fur, Jamie had remembered that brag from one of the kids. They went on to check their guns before putting all their items onto the quad bikes.

Jamie stood there, watching with bated breath as the three men rode towards the forest, and prayed that her dad's promise of coming back soon wasn't a lie this time.

CHAPTER 4

It had been three days.

Her dad wasn't back yet and neither were the men who'd gone out with their guns. She only knew that last fact because, every so often, she would see Dr Cora standing outside the lab staring at the mountain. Waiting.

Cora would stand there for a long time until one of her white-coated lackeys would come and get her for something.

As Jamie watched her watch the mountainside, she came to realise that the men out hunting were sent by Cora. Which meant that now, more than ever, Artemis was in danger. And her dad was nowhere in sight.

She had tried to call him on the satellite phone he'd left her, "in case of emergencies" he'd said, but each time she'd called he hadn't answered. What was the point of telling her to use it in an emergency if he wasn't there to receive the emergence?

On the fourth day, Jamie had been sent out to the market to grab some fruits and meat for her auntie. She'd been told off for pacing too much in the house and was sent to do some chores to stop her wearing a hole into the floor.

It was while she was there, ignoring the biting words of the nearby kids and their parents, that she heard the hollering.

The growls of an engine being revved echoed into the air echoed all around, swallowed immediately by the cheers of the three men that rode the four-wheeled machines. One held his gun high in the air, stood up on the bike as it rolled to a stop. The other two followed closely behind, yelling just as loudly and excitedly.

Jamie was nervous to go closer. There was a large group of people surrounding the men, cheering along with them. The people here hated her; getting too close could be a problem.

But her anxiety about why they were so happy forced her to walk towards them, keeping enough of a distance to be out of sight. She was glad she'd kept that distance when she caught sight of the blood. The sight of it alone nearly made her gag.

There, strung across the leather of the first man's bike seat, was a dead wolf.

Its eyes were open wide, glassy and dead. It looked as if the poor creature had died of shock, its tongue hanging listlessly from the open mouth, spattered with blood. The once beautiful grey fur was now covered in its own blood and matted with mud and snow from where, Jamie could only assume, it had been drug across the ground.

"That'll teach them!" one person from the crowd cried, gleeful.

One of the men, the one who had led the group into the town, stepped towards the wolf and leant against the quad bike, smiling as someone took a photo of him with the dead animal.

"Found this beast close to the mountains, probably after our sheep again."

An angry grumble grew among the crowd; Jamie could only assume that they had experience with wolves going after their animals. That didn't make sense though. Wolves avoided people as much as they could, unless they were desperate.

"We'll show them," the hunter cried, raising his gun high, "no wolves in Materia!"

"No more wolves in Materia!" the people chorused.

Jamie didn't stick around after that.

Her dad needed to know what was happening here. Artemis and the wolves were in danger, and he was their only hope. She wouldn't stop calling until he answered.

CHAPTER 5

"Jamie-bear, I'm sorry I haven't taken your calls..." William started, his voice distant, distracted. "There were a lot more complications here than I realised—"

"They killed a wolf, Daddy," Jamie said, interrupting, her voice sounding so much younger than usual. Like she was on the edge of tears. "They're going to kill them all." She choked on a sob then.

She didn't realise just how scared she was until the tears started to fall, making it hard for her to breathe. This wasn't the first time she'd seen a dead animal, not that her dad knew that. The first time was when she was five. Her mum had forgotten to pack away the pictures from their trip before letting Jamie use the office for her homework. She knew what a dead wolf looked like.

Seeing one in the flesh though? It was more terrifying than she expected. Looking into the eyes of an intelligent creature, cut down so cruelly and unfairly, and seeing nothing reflected back, hurt. Seeing the stiffness of its body, the muscles contracted tightly as if the wolf had tried to run away only to then die in excruciating pain. Pain was all Jamie could see when she saw that beautiful wolf's body.

Jamie couldn't get the picture out of her head.

"Daddy, what do I do?" she cried, her eyes stinging with tears, her nose dribbling with snot that she brushed away with the back of her hand.

The phone stayed silent.

Pulling the phone away from her ear, Jamie worried that she'd lost the connection to her dad, then she heard his voice come through again.

"I'm coming to you."

Jamie didn't respond, too stunned by the change in his tone. He sounded angry, though that word didn't seem strong enough. She heard him shouting at someone in the background. The phone microphone wasn't sensitive enough to pick up what he was saying, but the viciousness in his voice was enough to keep Jamie silent.

Then he came back to her.

"Sweetheart, I know you're hurting over what you saw, but I need you to wait for me. Don't go outside. Don't engage with anyone. Don't even tell auntie that you told me about this, okay?"

She swallowed and nodded, then realised he couldn't see that.

"Okay…"

"I'll be with you soon, I prom—" He stopped short, as if remembering what he'd said days ago. "I'll be there soon, okay?"

Jamie didn't have time to answer before he hung up on her. Putting the phone down, she frowned, wondering what he was planning. All she could think about was what he'd said when he answered.

Their plan wasn't working out.

Is that why he's coming home so easily? Jamie wondered as she laid back on her bed, turning her head to look at Artemis' cat. *He's never come home when I've been sad before.*

Hours passed and nothing changed.

She didn't hear from her dad again nor could she get in touch with him when she tried to ring again. Jamie had done what he'd said and not left the house, but she'd spied out the windows just in case. That's when she saw the hunters preparing to go out once more.

One was cleaning the blood off their bikes while another was packing bags with survival items, and lots of ammunition. The one that had their photo taken with the dead wolf was cleaning the guns, a disgustingly big grin on his face.

Jamie tried to call her dad, but he didn't pick up.

Frustration built in her stomach. She couldn't just stand by and watch them ride off to kill another wolf. What if they hurt one of Artemis' family? Or hurt Artemis? Jamie couldn't let it happen.

So she took one of the knives from the kitchen, one with a sharp point, and put it in her coat pocket. She put on a pair of gloves and then tucked her hands into her pockets. With a deep breath, she disobeyed her dad's orders, and stepped outside.

A crowd had grown near the men. The excitement in the air was palpable at the possibility of another murder. Materia truly was a hateful place.

Using the big coat she'd put on before stepping out into the cold air to her advantage, Jamie hid herself beside the crowd, keeping the hood low over her face. Knife in hand, she came close to the last quad bike, the one without anyone nearby.

"Hey!" a gruff voice shouted, catching Jamie's attention just before a hand yanked off the hood on her head.

Jumping back in surprise, Jamie turned to see one of the hunters standing in front of her. He was so tall she had to lift her head high to look him in the face. His eyes were a harsh brown, dark, soulless, and his unshaven face was twisted into a scowl.

"What you doing, huh?" the man demanded, stepping closer, forcing Jamie to step backwards. "What d'ya want?"

The people there all turned towards Jamie, their glares making her sweat.

Jamie didn't have time to answer, she wasn't even sure what she would have said if she did, because a terrible screech of tyres drew everyone's attention away from her and towards the incoming car.

It came to a sliding halt in the snow and then, from the thrown-open door, came Jamie's dad. Immediately behind him, coming from the other side, another man stepped out. He looked important with his clean-shaven face, glasses, suit, and briefcase.

"What the..." The hunter stepped away from Jamie, to her relief, and headed towards her dad. "Oi, you can't park here."

As the hunter headed towards her dad and the locals turned away from her, Jamie slipped away and into the shadows of the nearest house, one that faced the lab's building. While there, she watched the scene in front of her, only just noticing the door of the lab opening and Dr Cora stepping out to watch as well.

Jamie scowled at the woman, not fully paying attention to her dad. This was the woman who'd caused all the trouble recently. The one who had probably sent the men out to

Swen Forest to hunt the wolves, and most likely to find Artemis too.

Dr Cora's head turned towards her then, staring directly at Jamie.

She smiled, showing off her teeth.

Jamie looked away, focusing back on her dad, though she could feel the doctor's gaze still on her. Thankfully, as her dad spoke, Jamie found herself able to ignore the feeling.

"There will be no more hunting in Materia," he said, his voice loud and clear, echoing across the street.

The hunter who'd grabbed Jamie stepped forward, getting into her dad's face, and growled out, "Who the hell do you think you are to demand that?"

"Me? Oh, I'm no one special." She may not have been able to see it, but Jamie could hear the smile in her dad's words. "Professor Johnson here, however, well, he's a very important man. Sir?"

Her dad stepped back, gesturing for the smartly dressed man to speak. Jamie frowned, unsure what was happening.

Professor Johnson opened his briefcase, and from it, he pulled a piece of paper, raising it above his head. In a projected voice, one he seemed to be used to using, the man spoke.

"I have here a signed executive order from the governor stating that the forest of Swen and the creatures within are to receive environmental protection against hunting." A collective grumble grew within the people. "For the next decade, no person may enter the forest with the intent of hunting. Nor can any harm or forced removal come to *any* of the creatures within its borders. Anyone who kills a creature will receive fines up to two thousand pounds."

The people of Materia understood what no hunting meant. And an uproar went up as the professor continued.

"Here is your copy of the order. You can vote to have it revoked in ten years time."

He held the document out to the hunter who refused to take it, rudely saying what he thought of his paper with words that, if Jamie had said them, she'd have been made to wash her mouth out with soap.

Professor Johnson handed the document to Jamie's dad who gave his thanks. The man then got back in the car, and after awkwardly reversing, he eventually left. Jamie watched the car fade into the distance, not able to process what had just happened when her dad turned up at her side, taking her hand in his.

As he pulled her away quickly, trying to get them away from the angry mob, Jamie looked back to Dr Cora.

Under her armpit was the paper Jamie's dad had taken. She was looking at Jamie, her smile just as wide and cruel as she clapped in her direction.

Jamie had won this round against the doctor. Yet, as her dad dragged her into the house, it didn't feel much like a victory. She could only hope ten years would be enough to plan what to do next to keep Artemis safe.

She would protect Artemis and the wolves.

Always.

EPILOGUE

$\mathcal{L}$ife in Materia was uncomfortable after what happened. Not that Jamie minded much. The place had been a nightmare ever since she arrived; this was really no different from before – except when the people would come to the house demanding answers. That, Jamie admitted, was a little scary.

Her aunt wasn't exactly thrilled to have them here either, not that they had much choice. Her and her dad didn't have anywhere to go. They did have their own house on the other, but they hadn't been there in years. Ever since her mum had died. Adding to that, the house was an ocean's distance away from here. Jamie could hardly imagine leaving this place, as much as she hated it, and abandoning Artemis. What if Artemis came looking for her and she wasn't here?

There's no point going home anyway, she thought bitterly, watching as her dad paced back and forth while speaking animatedly with someone on the phone. Her dad would leave soon after, like he always did, and she would be dropped off like luggage with someone she didn't know, like she always was. Jamie was sick of it. She may be young, but just as her dad had shown her these last few weeks, she deserved better.

"Thanks, Roger, I can be packed and out of here in a few days. Can you get the tickets booked?"

Jamie scowled. She hated that he'd proved her bitter thoughts right.

No, she thought, her resolve hardening. *No, not this time.*

Her dad looked at her out of the corner of his eye and threw her a smile before focusing back on the call.

"Thursday at five p.m.? Sounds good. See you soon, Roger. Bye. Bye."

Hanging up the phone and placing it on the table in front of him, her dad turned to her, eyebrow raised. With a motion of his head to the nearby armchair, he took his spot on the floor in front of it.

Jamie held back a smile. At least he was getting better at recognising when she wanted to say something.

Taking a seat in the chair, wiggling her butt to get comfortable, she straightened her shoulders to look as grown up as possible. The effect wasn't the easiest to maintain considering her feet couldn't reach the floor.

"I have choices for you," she said, threading her fingers together like she saw on those spy shows.

He just nodded his head, giving her permission to carry on. His smile never left.

"I miss mum," Jamie started, frowning, not sure why she started there. "And I miss you too. So take me with you." Her dad went to interrupt her, but she glared at him. "Or we go home. Our real home. You teach people and me, and we aren't..." She waved her arms trying to find the right word. "...gone anymore."

Jamie leant back against the back of the chair then,

crossing her arms. She hoped that her grown-up serious expression was enough to show how determined she was.

Her dad just watched her for a moment, his thinking face in full use as he tilted his head to the side. He reminded her of the puppy her mum had nearly bought her before she died. The image of her dad as a puppy made her smile, until she remembered she was meant to be looking serious.

"I will take option B, Miss Gander-Yoon."

Jamie deflated instantly. She shouldn't have been surprised; of course he wouldn't choose her over his—

Wait, Jamie's mind raced as she sat up quickly. *Did he...?*

"You..." she started, unbelieving. "You'll stay with me?"

Leaning forward, laying his hand on her knee as he often did, his blue eyes held her brown. His smile was soft, if a little sad, as if he knew what she had been thinking.

"I should have chosen you a long time ago, Jamie," he said, his words soft. "Better late than a zero, as your mum used to say."

Tears built in Jamie's eyes.

"You're staying?" she asked again.

He reached a hand up to her cheek, brushing away a tear that had fallen.

"We're going home."

THINGS MOVED QUICKLY AFTER THAT. TURNS OUT that the Roger her dad had been talking to was actually getting him tickets to go home. It rather took the taste of her victory, but she couldn't stop smiling when she heard he'd already planned to never leave her again.

"Roger works for the university near the house. I'll be able to go back to teaching, and if you're good," he said with a smile, nudging her with his foot, making her giggle, "I may sneak you into some of my classes. Only way to learn more about Artemis and her family is through a good ol' anthrozo-ology education."

Jamie had no idea what any of that meant, but the fact that it would mean she could learn more to help Artemis was the only thing that mattered.

"I'll be an anth-ruh-zoo-log-ist when I'm older, then," she said matter-of-factly as she gently put her cat toy into her suitcase, before taking it out again to put in the satchel her dad had given her last night.

As she looked at the toy, whose head was poking out the flap of the satchel, she didn't want it to suffocate after all, she thought about Artemis and the wolves more. Worry grew in her stomach.

"Artemis will be okay without me here, right?"

Her dad stopped packing and turned to her, surprised. Coming to her side and dropping down to one knee, he laid a hand on her shoulder.

"Jamie-bear, you have done more for that girl than she may ever know. All you can do now is learn as much as you can to use that to help Artemis and her pack in the future." He squeezed her shoulder affectionately. "We have ten years until we have to start worrying. Use that time."

Pressing a kiss to her forehead, he went back to finish his packing.

Jamie wished she could be reassured that easily. She knew there wasn't much she could do as a ten-year-old. She'd learnt that much these last few weeks. But she couldn't stand the idea of leaving Artemis behind. Even if the wolf-girl didn't know she'd gone, Jamie would.

She wasn't sure what she was going to do until her dad was loading their things into the taxi he'd called.

Turning away from the car, Jamie turned and ran for the hill. The hill where she'd said goodbye to the girl she'd saved. The hill where she'd cried harder than she'd ever done before. The hill where she saw the wolf-girl she loved disappear into her forest.

Sweating and her chest heaving, Jamie stood next to the sheep pen, staring up at the mountains and the grove of trees that lined its entrance.

"Before I go, Artemis, I want you to know," Jamie started, her words heavy and filled with promise. "I will come back to you one day. One day we'll be together again. I swear."

Taking a breath, Jamie turned away and headed back to the car where her dad waited, smiling proudly.

Jamie smiled back.

FINDING HOME

FRANCESCA MCMAHON

CHAPTER 1

The human world was strange. Not necessarily in a bad way, but she was unsure if she could see it in a good way either.

It had only been a few weeks since Artemis had left the Forest to be with her Jamie, and she had already seen so much of the human world that she could hardly understand. Luckily, Artemis had always been a curious explorer.

The first place she found herself with her new pack was a strange and extravagant Den named "ho-tell". The place was like nothing she'd ever seen. Though, being from the Forest, that was the case with much of the human world. From high walls to bright, sunlight-coloured skies and an unknowable number of doors, Artemis was awestruck. Unfortunately, so were the people when they first saw Artemis in her barely-there bottom fur. As she came to realise, that wasn't the appropriate thing for humans. They like to cover themselves up almost completely. Humans were very strange.

So, next came new fur. Lots of new furs. Or "clothes", as

Jamie said they were called. Artemis wasn't a fan. She hadn't minded wearing them when they had belonged to Jamie; her scent of pine and lavender had been ingrained into the material, making them comfortable to wear. These clothes weren't the same as that. These ones smelled of falsities. A scent so unnatural that the first time Artemis tried them on, she quickly tore off the material, the ingrained scent too bitter to her nose.

Eventually she settled on lots of loose-fitted furs of various types of grey. It made her feel connected to the wolf within her as well as her pack in the Forest. The colours so similar to their own fur that it was as if she were still with them.

Clothing had been an interesting experience to get used to, but she had, to an extent at least. After all that, her biggest experience since leaving the Forest came in the form of a large metal water box.

They didn't stay at the ho-tell very long. She and the pack were on the move not long after staying there. Jamie had stated that they would be travelling to her home via a metal box that she called a "bote". This boat began a journey across a vast river that she could never see the end of. She was told it was called the ocean, but she liked thinking of it more as a big river. It felt more normal to her that way. Artemis had never known a world larger than the Forest and the human town. It felt unnatural to her to see something so unending. Everything had an end. It was why the packs had territories. Jamie promised to show her a map of the world when they got home. Artemis wasn't sure she wanted to see it. The world was too big already.

When Elder Will had suggested watching the large river flow so she could see their journey progress, Artemis had agreed. She knew she'd have to learn about the strange ways of human travel eventually, and Elder Will always seemed ready to teach. Even if his methods were more stories than teaching. In this case, his story included a boy named Jack and a girl named Rose. Jamie and Ritchie found the chosen tale to be amusing, especially when Elder Kat jumped in to mention a specific door that appeared to frustrate the man if his angry huffs and puffs meant anything.

They were not long into their boat journey when Artemis's stomach started to hurt. In the end, she didn't spend much time looking out at the large river or listening to Elder Will's tales. Instead she found herself curling up with Jamie, her head tucked into her chest as she whined about the sickness growing within her stomach.

They were on the floating monster for days, and Artemis never felt any better. Jamie never left her side throughout. They were sharing a room with Ritchie, and so, if the need arose for food or water, Jamie would send him out on errands to get them. She'd once tried to go herself, but Artemis didn't want to be alone. So Jamie stayed by her side. Artemis was grateful, if a little embarrassed about her neediness. Rae had always told her she was a menace when she was feeling sick. Thankfully, Jamie didn't seem to mind.

The two of them ended up spending those days in the small bed talking and sleeping. Jamie talked all about her life in the human world. Her likes, dislikes, what she spent her time doing, and even about things she hoped Artemis would like about her world.

"I don't know," Jamie said with the most beautiful laugh Artemis had ever heard, "I just think you might like it."

"A bike?"

Jamie rolled onto her back and covered her eyes with her hand. "Ignore me, I think the sea air is getting to me."

With a cheeky smile, Artemis rolled towards and on top

of Jamie and pulled her hand away from her eyes, staring down at those wide open and bright oak-browns that looked up at hers. "Tell me."

"I-I, uh..." Jamie swallowed. "No?" she said in question, her eyes briefly dropping down to Artemis's lips and then back up to her eyes, so quickly that only an untrained eye wouldn't have noticed. But Artemis was a wolf. And wolves saw everything.

Artemis lent in closer, holding back a smile to keep up her serious act. "Tell. Me."

Jamie's eyes dropped to her lips again, this time much more noticeable than before, as she swallowed deeply. Artemis could see her chest rising and falling faster as she answered.

"Well, I-I thought you'd like to be able to be as fast as your family." She licked her lips.

Jamie wanted Artemis to still be connected to her family, even if it was in a somewhat human way. Just hearing her say that made Artemis love her all the more.

"A-A bike can do that. You with, like, a faux leather jacket, jeans, and a bike would be—"

Artemis kissed her.

She felt Jamie smile against her lips. When a hand reached up to stroke her cheek as they kissed, Artemis knew they wouldn't be talking for a while.

When the two of them finally came up for air and snuggled in closely together, Artemis's mind ran a span a minute. Nothing seemed right about this world, and as her stomach churned from the movement of the boat once more, it seemed her body agreed. Artemis began questioning her decision to leave home. At home she had a place. Here...

"Will I fit?" she asked quietly.

Jamie pulled her in tighter and pressed a deep kiss against her temple.

"I hope so."

69

CHAPTER 2

They were on the boat for seven passes of the sun. Artemis never got used to the feeling in her stomach. When they stepped off the boat and onto land again, she was as wobbly and vulnerable as a newborn deer.

Artemis hated the boat, but as they moved farther away from it and became swallowed by the large crowds outside, Artemis had to stop herself from running back to it.

It was overwhelming. Everything was just too much. Colours everywhere, bright, dull, and mixed together. New smells combined to make a toxic scent of chemicals, burning food, and body odour. And the noise. The noise surrounded Artemis, swirling around her and seeping into her very bones until she couldn't move.

Artemis stopped in the middle of the path. Humans brushed up against her, knocking her out of their way or shouting at her for not moving. Her chest grew tight as she stared at her overbearing surroundings. From large, wooden Dens that housed the burning food smells to the packs of people that lined up in front of them, shouting towards the humans inside.

She could smell the burning taste of meat, though each sniff was different. One bitter, another sweet, while others wafted the aroma of fat that had Artemis shaking her head from the intensity. The sizzling, bubbling and chopping of each prepared meal echoed all around her, blending in with the endless chatter of the crowd. As they walked past, each cook yelled out to them and others, shouting louder and louder, trying to outdo one another.

It was too much.

A hand touched her bicep, and she yelped in terror. She turned to find Jamie at her side, her hands raised in a placating manner.

"It's OK," Jamie said in a gentle voice barely audible above the noise. "Come on, we'll get out of here."

Jamie called out to Elder Will, Elder Kat, and Ritchie to come closer and, like a pack of wolves protecting an injured member, they surrounded her and began to march forward. Jamie wrapped an arm around Artemis's shoulder and urged them on through the crowd. Before, they had dodged and weaved through the crowd, being mindful of others. Now the three members of her pack strode forward, forcing the other humans to move out the way or be run down. They stayed close to her and Jamie, shielding Artemis from the crowds.

Eventually the intensity of the crowds and smells lessened as they moved farther and farther away from the dock. When they reached the edge, Elder Will quickly disappeared back into the crowds to fetch the car they had used to get to the boat. Artemis was about as comfortable with the car as she was the boat, but if it meant getting away from there, she could handle it.

It didn't take long for Elder Will to return with the car and for them all to be ushered inside. Only then did Artemis finally take a relaxed breath. She didn't let go of Jamie though; instead, she buried her face in the crook of her neck.

Artemis took a deep breath, drinking in the scent that was all Jamie. Pine, lavender, and something that was just *her*. She never moved away from her throughout the rest of the journey to her new home. Afraid of what the outside may hold.

WHAT ARTEMIS HAD HOPED WOULD BE A ONE-OFF experience of overload on her senses ended up being far more common than she expected.

Lights were too bright, noises were much louder, night wasn't truly night, and, to make things worse, there was no Forest. Or at least, none that deserved the name of such.

It had only been half a moon cycle after they arrived that Jamie had taken them to what she had called a park. They'd gone when the sun was at its highest, a time that Jamie said would be with less people due to something called "skool". In the end, the lack of humans made no difference to Artemis's comfort.

This false Forest was an open field, little to no trees, and a strange climbing area with fake tree bark and grass across its ground. Calling it a forest felt like a mockery to her home. They didn't stay long there, as much as Jamie tried to encourage Artemis to give it a try.

Artemis had wanted to, had even run a circuit like she was doing a territory patrol at home, but it just didn't feel right. Especially in the new shoes she had been provided.

Jamie had warned her that the land here wasn't as safe as it was in the Forest to go barefoot. Artemis hated them but wore them for Jamie's sake.

Nothing in this new world felt right, but at least Jamie was there. She could work to be comfortable if it meant she got to stay with her.

CHAPTER 3

$\mathcal{A}$rtemis had been trying to fit in for the few months she'd been in the human world. It hadn't been easy, but she'd found ways to be at peace there. Most of which had been at Jamie's side at the "uni-verse-tea".

She'd joined her in the "lieberry" as she'd worked to finish her paper. They spent hours in that place. Artemis would often spend her time there watching Jamie work. Her tongue would poke out past her lips while her glasses slowly slid down her nose as her long fingers tapped quickly on the laptop. It had been fascinating and enthralling to examine her. When Artemis eventually got restless, she would venture into the lieberry itself. Strangely, unlike the park Jamie had taken her to, this place felt more like a forest. The smell of wood was strong, if a little disconcerting given the lack of trees themselves. With how enclosed and high the space was, Artemis found herself getting lost in the place. There was a lot to see, and though she couldn't yet read, she found herself picking up a few of the books that looked inviting with the hope she could learn.

Elder Will had even taken on the responsibility of teaching her to read in the evenings with the books she had chosen. It was a slow process, but she could see herself improving already.

Only a few weeks after Jamie had finished her paper and her lessons with Elder Will had begun, a rite of passage was organised for Jamie's work. Elder Will had called it a "grad-u-ation cer-e-money", but Artemis liked her word more. At the rite of passage, Jamie would receive a piece of paper for her hard work. Jamie had said it was what the paper represented that made it important, but Artemis hadn't really understood why. She felt proud of her either way and told her as much.

Then the rite of passage began and, to Artemis's surprise, being surrounded by an audience of hundreds was not as overwhelming as it had once been.

She sat with Ritchie at her side, his presence calming enough to keep any possible anxious energy within her at bay. Ahead, on the stage, sat Elder Will, Elder Kat and a few other humans that Artemis did not care to know. Eventually a parade of figures in strange all-black floor-length outfits walked on to shake hands with an older male and receive the important paper. It was rather tedious, but Artemis waited patiently for Jamie to arrive.

Jamie hadn't appeared yet when it happened.

A hand tapped at her shoulder, startling her from her concentration on finding Jamie. Turning, she met an inquisitive stare of a young blonde female with blue eyes who was staring at her in a way that made Artemis uncomfortable.

"You're her, right?" The girl lent in closer, drawing the attention of the one beside her. "That feral woman from the documentary?"

Artemis frowned, unsure how to respond. Thankfully, Ritchie intervened.

"No talking during the ceremony," he said in a quiet yet sharp voice as he stretched his arm around the back of Artemis's chair.

The next few moments passed by with no consequence, or at least, that's how it appeared.

A buzz in her ears alerted Artemis to what was happening behind her as the sound of whispers grew. Soon enough, it seemed everyone in proximity knew who she was. She tried to concentrate on what was happening on the stage, but as the chatter grew louder, others started to turn towards the building commotion. Even those on stage, including Elder Will and Elder Kat.

Artemis dug her nails into her palms, desperate to keep herself calm. She could feel her heartbeat rising as more eyes fell on her. The voices of the humans around her grew louder.

A pale hand dropped onto her shoulder from behind and, in her surprise, she lashed out with her nails, scratching deeply into the soft skin that held onto her. When the shrill scream hit her ears, Artemis realised what she had done.

The blonde cried out in pain as she jumped up from her chair, holding her bleeding hand in the other. "What the hell, you psycho!"

Ritchie was on his feet in an instant. "Hey, you were the one putting your hands on her," he snapped. "Did your mother never teach you to keep your hands to yourself?"

Everyone was watching them now. Artemis could feel their stares boring deep into her skin. It made her itch.

"The bitch attacked me!" the blonde squealed, her voice so high that Artemis couldn't help but flinch. "She should be locked up!"

Artemis didn't hear anything else after that. Standing from her seat quickly, barely glancing at Ritchie as he spoke her name or the voice of her soul calling out to her from the stage, she did what she had always done best.

She ran.

***

ARTEMIS'S SHOE-COVERED FEET POUNDED AGAINST the hard ground, sending uncomfortable vibrations up her legs as each foot hit the concrete. Eventually, Artemis stopped to remove the shoes, taking to running barefoot as she always had. She went to throw away the horrible contraptions, but in the end, she continued running with them in her hands.

Jamie had bought them for her not long after they got here. She'd let Artemis choose them of course; she always let Artemis choose. It was Jamie's way of helping her feel like she had a say over her life here. The shoes were a bright white colour, like her mother Larka's paws, and Artemis loved them. Even if they were uncomfortable to wear sometimes.

As Artemis ran, that day played over in her mind.

That day was the happiest she'd been since arriving in this new world. She and Jamie had ventured out to what she had called a shopping centre, and though it had been busy, Artemis found herself able to cope with the noise. All day Artemis and Jamie had explored that place and bought new things. From clothes of her usual greys, whites and browns for her wolf-self and all of the thin, tight material to keep her comfortable. As she shopped, as Jamie had called it, she'd felt Jamie watching her bounce around the store in amusement.

While wandering around, something unexpected caught Artemis's eye. Without thinking, she rushed off towards it, Jamie calling after her as she went. Coming to an abrupt halt outside a shop, Artemis leant against the window, her hands pressing hard against the glass as her eyes roamed the item inside it.

It was silver in colour, like the shine of moonlight, and reflected the sun in a way that made it gleam. The tiny chain links locked together intricately as it lay around a false neck with a singular silver pendant in its centre that, as Artemis looked closer, glittered in a way that kept her from looking away.

Until Jamie appeared.

Artemis pretended to be looking at something else when she asked her what she'd seen, though she wasn't sure why. It wasn't until they returned back to the house that Artemis found herself thinking of the "necklace", as Jamie had called them, and her desperate desire to have it. Not for her, but for Jamie. She just had to figure out how.

It had taken until this day, the day of Jamie's graduation, the day of most importance to her, for Artemis to collect it. Ritchie had helped her, having taken her to the shop and helped her figure out how to buy the necklace and wrap it in a small velvet box that tucked into her jacket pocket.

There had been a plan. One with flowers and alone time together where Artemis would present her this gift, place it around her neck, and tell her again how much Jamie meant to her.

Now, as her feet crashed against the hard ground, her jacket billowing behind her as she sped through the streets with a box in her pocket, she would never get to.

You never belonged here, a voice in her mind told her as the tears that had been brewing for months finally fell. *And now Jamie will know too.*

Artemis kept running with one place in mind. A place that would take her far from this world she didn't belong in.

CHAPTER 4

*H*er dad had wanted to get the police involved. The drama with the blonde, a woman by the name of Whitney, had eventually blown over after her boyfriend had shown up in his cap and gown and told her she should have kept her hands to herself. One problem had been solved, but the other was ongoing. Artemis was missing.

"Dad, we can't call the cops. They won't know how to deal with her. They're more likely to hurt her than help her. You know what they're like." Jamie looked helplessly at her phone. She knew she should have pushed for Artemis to use one for whenever this happened. "She can't have gone far. She doesn't know the area that well. If the four of us work together, we…" Jamie trailed off and ran a hand through her hair.

"I'll call some of my film buddies," Ritchie said quietly. He'd been feeling awful ever since Artemis had run off, convinced that he should have done more to stop her or follow her. Jamie didn't blame him. Artemis was faster than lightning when she needed to be. "That'll add a few more people to the search party."

"And I'll speak to some of my contacts who were here for the ceremony," Alicaster said. "They saw what happened, they'll know how to approach her to not frighten her off."

"Yes, I'll make some calls also," her dad said with a nod. "And you were right about the police, Jamie. I wasn't thinking straight. We can do this ourselves, no police."

Jamie offered them all a smile of thanks. Taking off her glasses to rub her eyes, Jamie let out a heavy breath. "Let's try to find her before it gets dark."

That, of course, was easier said than done.

As it turned out, Artemis may have known the town better than Jamie expected. Either that, or she was following her instincts and was going off alone. Jamie prayed that it was the first one, at least in that case they had a chance of finding her.

When night came, Jamie desperately tried to convince her dad to let her keep searching, but as he pointed out, Artemis would do much better at night than Jamie could.

For the first time in months, Jamie found herself sleeping alone. She didn't realise how used to sleeping with Artemis in her arms she'd got until she was without her. Jamie tossed and turned for hours and attempted to use a pillow as an Artemis replacement until she eventually gave up and climbed out of bed to take a walk.

Jamie paced back and forth across the moonlit hallways of the upstairs floor, her bare feet pressing against the cool wood-panelled floors as she tried to exhaust herself into sleep. When that didn't work, she resigned herself to not sleeping and slunk down into the window seat and stared out into the night.

Curling her knees up into her chest and wrapping her

arms around them, Jamie leant her head against the window, wincing slightly at the cold before settling in. Outside in their small garden, Jamie watched as the swings on her old swing set swayed in the wind, and smiled.

Artemis had been fascinated by the swing, until she'd watch Jamie swing on it and then jump off. She went into full panic, checking Jamie over for injuries and growling at the swing. She'd been a little more forgiving of the seat when Jamie had her sit on it.

Turning away from the swings, Jamie leant her head against the wall behind her and sighed.

Why did Artemis run? she thought as she absentmindedly picked at the fraying hem of her pyjama bottoms. *Surely she knows I wouldn't be mad at her.*

Staring at the wall opposite her on the window ledge, Jamie thought back to the last time she and Artemis had sat here together. It was the day she'd taken Artemis out to the park, which unfortunately, left a lot to be desired for Artemis's need for nature. Artemis had been quiet ever since they'd come home that day, and Jamie had tried to think of a way to fix it.

That night, while sitting here at the window seat in the hallway, Jamie told Artemis of a forest that she wanted to take her to. One that was farther away from here, nearly an hour's drive, but was a place that was incredibly special to her.

"It's where my mum used to take me when I was a kid, and well, it became an even better place to go a few years ago." Jamie smiled as Artemis tugged at the edge of her pyjama bottoms where a loose thread lay. "It's not yet opened up properly to the public, but it will be soon, then we can go."

Artemis hadn't said anything, just hmm'd in response as

she tugged at the loose thread. Jamie had wondered if Artemis wasn't excited about the forest because of how far away she'd said it was, so she showed her a map on her phone. Still Artemis stayed quiet. They didn't move from the window seat for such a long time that Jamie almost fell asleep there, until Artemis spoke.

"I don't belong here…"

Jamie hadn't said anything. She'd sat there in silence, faking sleep against the windowsill, waiting to see if Artemis would say anything more. She didn't. Instead, she had come to Jamie's side and gently lifted her from the window seat to carry her to their bed.

Jamie continued to stay quiet as Artemis settled down on the bed in front of her. Only when Artemis fell still did Jamie move, pulling the woman's warm body against hers. Jamie dipped her nose into the soft brown hair at the nape of her neck and squeezed her tightly, hoping to convey in her movements the love she had for her. The belief she had that they could make this work.

Yet, Jamie never said a word. Never consoled her. Never told her that she was wrong and that she did belong. And look where that had gotten them.

"I'm sorry, Artemis," Jamie whispered as a tear trickled down her cheek.

She would fix the mess she'd made, she would—

Jamie sat up straight, nearly tumbling off the window seat in her haste. The forest she'd told Artemis about. She'd shown her the directions. They'd planned a whole trip to it.

Running towards her bedroom, she pulled out whatever clothes she could get her hands on and threw them on. Jamie grabbed her keys and ran out the front door towards her car.

It's possible that this was just a wild goose chase, but as

Jamie turned her ignition on, she didn't care. If there was any chance that Artemis was there, she was going to find her.

She would always find her.

CHAPTER 5

*J*amie knew she would have a speeding ticket with how fast she was going. Maybe five. But she didn't care as she continued to speed ahead with her headlights on full, searching for Artemis along the path to the forest.

She'd only been driving for about half an hour when she realised that Artemis would likely be following her wolf instincts and staying out of sight of the road as she walked. Jamie wouldn't be able to see her if she was off-path.

"Crap," she muttered as she pulled up onto the side of the road, flicking her hazards on. There was hardly anyone out at this time of night, but she didn't want to risk the chance of an officer driving past and looking for an easy target.

Getting out of her car, she started to call out for Artemis as she walked along the road, both in front and behind her car. When a few minutes passed and she had no response, she would get back in her car and drive ahead a few miles away and do the same.

Drive, stop, call, wait, drive, repeat.

Nearly two hours had passed, and Jamie had only made it about halfway towards the forest with this stop-and-start method, and in that time she hadn't seen a single sign of Artemis. Jamie smacked her steering wheel in frustration but continued driving. She couldn't give up now. She refused to.

As she pulled up on the side of the road again to step out and away from her car to call out for Artemis, she received no response. Sighing, Jamie turned back towards her car to move on when something caught her eye within the roadside trees.

She stumbled a little climbing over the barrier. Jamie used the glow of her headlights to watch where she was going. There, caught on a nearby tree branch, was a jacket. Artemis's jacket. The very one she'd been wearing earlier that day at Jamie's graduation.

Grabbing it off the branch, Jamie clutched it to her chest and desperately looked around in the darkness surrounding her for any other sign. It was below freezing, and while she knew Artemis could handle the cold, that didn't lessen her anxiety.

"Artemis!" she yelled, her voice cracking with the exertion. "Artemis, I'm here!"

Jamie waited longer than she had before, even wandering farther out into the dark, though not too deep into it that she lost the light of her car. Ten minutes of calling and waiting left Jamie rushing back towards the roadside barrier. If Artemis was nearby, she had to keep going to try and find her.

As she was climbing over the fence, she heard a small thud against the asphalt of the road. Using the headlights, Jamie reached down to find a velvet box. Her heart raced for a moment thinking something ridiculous but, after opening it with shaky fingers, she found a beautiful, embedded-silver crest necklace.

How did... She thought back to how Ritchie said he'd taken Artemis to the ceremony yesterday morning. *I can't believe it.*

Closing the box and tucking it back into the jacket pocket, she continued her way towards her car. Now wasn't the time to think about jewellery.

It was when she opened the driver's-side door that she heard it.

SNAP.

Jamie stood still, hand still on the door frame. No other sound followed, but Jamie knew what, or who, it was.

"Artemis," she said loud enough to be heard but gentle so as to not frighten. "It's OK. You can come down."

Not closing her door, afraid to spook her, Jamie turned towards the tree-line and waited at the side of the vehicle. As she hoped, Jamie heard the sound of creaking branches breaking through the stillness of the night. Jamie stared at the tree in front of her that the jacket had been found in.

Eventually, a pale leg appeared through the leaves, the glow of headlights reflecting off it easily. Jamie didn't move a muscle as, slowly, the rest of a body appeared. While the lights from the car didn't catch all of the woman, Jamie was able to make out enough to see the torn-up clothing she was wearing. She had to clench her hands to stop herself from moving forward.

"It's OK," Jamie whispered as Artemis skittered back and forth between the shadows of the tree and the silver metal barrier. "Take your time."

And she did. It was almost like they'd reverted back to their childhood, to the first time Jamie had found her locked up in the lab. She'd been patient then too, waiting for

Artemis to make the first moves, just as she did now. Jamie could feel the anxiety rolling of Artemis in waves. From her hunched shoulders, her inability to meet Jamie's eyes, and the cautiously small steps forwards that were quickly undone by large ones backwards.

"I'm here, Artemis. You're OK." She stood with her posture open and welcoming, her hands limp at her sides. "No one's going to hurt you."

It was as Artemis clamoured over the metal barrier, the shoes she'd been wearing held tightly in her grasp, that Jamie was able to fully see her. She had to blink away tears at the sight.

The outfit Artemis had worn at the ceremony was in tatters. From the long-sleeved shirt being split and frayed in more than one area to her bare feet covered in mud and blood. Unlike the world Artemis grew up in, the ground here was not often safe to walk on barefooted, from broken glass bottles to untrodden sharp rock, there were an untold number of problems. Artemis had learnt that the hard way if the still-dripping cuts were anything to go by. Even her hands and face, both of which had historical scars, had new scratches to add to its collection. Artemis didn't meet her gaze as she stepped closer.

"Are you OK?" Jamie asked quietly, not daring to reach a hand out to touch her, not yet.

"I—" Artemis started, her voice tight. "I'm sorry, Jamie…"

Tears finally slipped down Jamie's cheek at those three words.

Artemis sounded so *broken*. Everything about her looked closed off as she wrapped her arms tightly around herself. She couldn't even look Jamie in the eye. Like she was resigned to her fate. What she thought that fate was, Jamie had no idea.

Jamie's initial relief at seeing the woman she loved turned rapidly into exhaustion. An exhaustion she felt awful about.The fear and sorrow in Artemis's eyes reminded Jamie so much of the days after Cora's cruelty against her. Her muscles were taut as she curled in on herself, like she was preparing for the next lashing. Jamie knew she could run again at any moment.

And Jamie would be damned if she ever let Artemis fall back so far.

"No, Artemis." Jamie stepped forward. "You've no reason to—"

Those green eyes finally looked at her. Dried tears marked her dirty face as new ones followed the ready-made path down the grime. Her green eyes shone with fresh tears, and her lip trembled.

"I don't belong here."

Jamie couldn't stop herself. She rushed forward and pulled Artemis into the tightest hug she possibly could. Artemis's face fell into the nape of her neck, her tears soaking Jamie's shirt in seconds.

"This is not your fault, Artemis," Jamie said through her own tears. "None of what happened is your fault." Pulling back, she took Artemis's face in her hands and brushed away the tears there. "You aren't in trouble, and you don't need to run away. I was never going to be mad at you."

"Space…" Artemis whispered, dropping Jamie's gaze. "Need space."

Jamie stepped back from her, giving exactly what she needed. She waited for the woman to look up at her again and offered her a small smile. "Can I show you something?"

CHAPTER 6

Artemis silently stared out the car window. She watched as tree after tree passed the car by and let the soft lull of music from Jamie's "ray-dio" fill the silence.

When she'd first run from the ceremony, she'd not known where she wanted to go. Only when she found herself running alongside the road in the direction of the forest that Jamie had shown her did she know. It made sense in her mind to go there. Jamie had said it would be the perfect place to find a home away from home. Artemis only ran into problems with getting there when some angry human cars started loudly growling at her when she'd first started running along the road. She'd moved to the woods by the roadside soon after to avoid them.

Artemis wasn't sure when or why she'd climbed the tree. All she could remember was feeling tired of it all. Tree-climbing had been something she had loved doing back home, whether it be for survival or to find a quiet place to just be, it was what helped her. She'd hung her jacket up for safekeeping before climbing, but with how easily Jamie had found her, Artemis half wished she hadn't. Jamie would be better off if she hadn't.

Artemis's fingers rubbed against an ache in her chest as she held back a sigh.

"We're nearly there," Jamie's voice broke through her haze. "Hold on a little longer, OK?"

She didn't say a word, afraid of what Jamie may think if she said what she'd been feeling since she'd set foot on that boat. This world did not want her. The ceremony incident, while the final straw, wasn't the first thing that had told Artemis she wasn't made for this place.

Instead, Artemis reached out a hand and rested it beside Jamie on her chair. She didn't turn to look at her, couldn't, but she needed to be near her. She loved being near and being held by Jamie. She loved Jamie in a way that she had never loved before. Being with her made her think of the stories and feelings Kiba had told her about him and Rae.

Whenever she is near, he had said in that wistful way he always did when speaking of Rae, **I know everything is going to be fine even if I do not know what is to come.**

Everything made sense when Artemis was with Jamie. Except for this world. How could she be the one for Jamie when nothing about Artemis fit in the world that was her home?

She'd be better off without me here, Artemis thought as she moved her hand away from Jamie's side.

Or at least, that's what she tried to do when a warm grip fell around her wrist. Finally, she turned towards the woman beside her and found her still staring. Jamie's grip was firm, just as it had been on the wheel in front of her. She smiled. "We're here."

Artemis turned to stare out the front window and, though it was pitch black, the lights from the car and the moon above were enough to illuminate the sight in front of them. Farther than the eye could see, spreading across the horizon and up and down hills, was a forest. Trees and bushes ranged in height and size, species and placement, and some were even the same as home. There were a few that were in bloom from the warmer weather while others were slower in their growth and only showed small signs of change.

"This is the Remembered Wood." Jamie turned off the growl of the engine. "Come on, I've got something to show you."

Letting go of her wrist, Jamie opened the door and exited the vehicle. Artemis, after a moment's hesitation, did the same. Jamie came to her side and, with a hand hovering over Artemis's lower back, guided them towards the entrance of the forest. Artemis couldn't help but look up in awe as they began walking through.

"This place has been in progress for a few years. Trees take a long time to grow. Who knew?" Jamie laughed. "The owner is a big environmentalist, and he's been working to create a fully green-belt area for the city but with a twist.

"Each tree represents a life. Some will have plaques on the trees themselves" – she pointed to one with a gleaming shine in the trunk – "and others will have little memorial stones on the ground next to them." She pointed to one with a small headstone that rested against the sticking-out roots of an oak. "Best part about this place, each memorial can be erected for free. No worries for costs of the plaques at all. Only thing the owner, Mr Chase, asks is if you can donate some money, please do."

Artemis broke away from Jamie when she caught sight of one tree plaque. The silver stood out against the brown of the bark in a way that, though it should be jarring, fit with the world around it. She'd not learnt to read well yet, but as she brushed her fingers against the cool material, a gentle smile slipped across her lips.

"It's amazing, right?" Jamie said, her voice little more than a whisper. Artemis turned to her with a frown. There was something different in her tone now, a sort of sadness that hadn't been there before. Jamie gestured ahead of them. "There's one in particular I want to show you."

Artemis came to her side and, sensing a weight on the woman's shoulders, she slipped a hand into hers and held on tightly. Jamie offered her a grateful smile and kept moving. Artemis wondered how she was able to find her way so easily; her eyesight wasn't as strong as hers, yet she had been able to guide them with purpose.

It wasn't long until they came to a stop around the twelfth row of trees and moved into the row towards the fourth trunk with a silver "plak" on it. Unlike the others they'd seen walking past, this plak had an additional design.

"Wolf," Artemis said loudly in surprise.

"Yeah, a wolf." Artemis turned towards her and watched, stunned, as a singular tear slipped down Jamie's cheek. "Dad said it's what she would have wanted. She'd often say, 'I didn't get a PhD to not live and die with wolves,' so it felt fitting that she'd be with them even here."

Artemis turned back to the tree and took a solitary step forward. Reaching a hand up, Artemis traced her fingers across the lines of the wolf and the letters on the cool metal.

"Mother," Artemis said, glancing at Jamie over her shoulder. "Your mother?"

Jamie nodded and stepped forward to be beside Artemis. "Hi, Mum, I—" She choked back a sob that had Artemis leaning in closer to her, offering what little comfort her presence could. "I brought someone to meet you."

Artemis smiled her wide smile at the tree. "Hello. I am

Artemis." She touched a finger to the marking of the wolf. "My family in other place too."

Jamie leant heavily against Artemis's side as she silently cried. Artemis held her hand tighter.

"I miss them," Artemis said quietly. "Missing hard. You know them, but they gone." Her eyes started to water, and she swallowed. "I miss more here. It hard here. I do not…" She wracked her brain for the word she wanted. "I do not fit." Home I had place. Here it…different."

Jamie stood up, drawing Artemis's attention towards her. Her red eyes glimmered with heartbreak. "I knew you were struggling, I just didn't know…"

"It okay, I not know too."

A hand fell against her cheek. "You don't have to hide these things from me or from yourself. It'll be hard" – Jamie shook her head – "and I'm sorry I didn't help prepare you better for this. But I am here for you, and this wood is here for you too."

"What do you mean?" Artemis asked.

"This place opens to the public soon, but I doubt it'll be busy all the time. If you ever need a place to escape the loudness of the world, you can come here. I'll show you the safer way to get here so you don't have to rely on me, or hurt your feet." She gestured to her mother's tree. "You can keep Mum company and tell her your worries." Jamie smiled. "I did it all the time when she was around and even after she'd gone. She's a pretty good listener."

"You…" Artemis started, "you do that?"

Jamie leant forward, and with only a pause to silently ask for permission, she pressed her lips gently to Artemis's. Warmth flowed through her body at the touch, and in response, Artemis leant in deeper. Eventually they pulled away, breathless.

"I love you, Artemis. I would do anything to make sure you are happy here." Jamie's smile faltered slightly. "Even if it means taking you back. We can compromise, I'm sure—"

Artemis kissed her again.

"No," she said sternly after. "I want…just need time."

"Always," Jamie replied, her thumb rubbing against Artemis's cheek. "And if you do ever—"

"I will tell."

They stood silently there for a moment until something dawned on Artemis. Reaching for the jacket still in Jamie's hand, she pulled out the soft box she had collected with Ritchie yesterday out of its pocket. She knew that Jamie had already seen it, she'd watched the whole thing from her tree.

"This was for your…" Artemis paused on the word, still unsure of the pronunciation. "For your day."

Artemis opened the box and pulled out the necklace that Ritchie had called "cri-stal" when she'd shown him. What had made the necklace stand out to Artemis was the shape. Though she couldn't know for sure, the thick lines and the fall of the branches, she was sure it was an oak tree. An oak tree for the girl who had once been her Oak.

Without a word, Jamie turned and tugged her hair aside. Artemis stepped forward and dropped the necklace around Jamie's neck and, with only a minor struggle, clasped the ends together.

Jamie pressed her fingers to the necklace as she turned to face her. "It's beautiful."

"Like you," Artemis replied.

The two shared another kiss. It was brief and yet it meant everything. Every fear, every worry, every love, every thought, it was all within that kiss.

And now it was time to leave.

When the two began walking, Artemis paused and

glanced back at the tree. "See you…" She looked at Jamie, a silent question passing between them.

"Seon-mi."

"See you, Seon-mi," Artemis said.

With Jamie's hand in hers, the two of them left the woods with the light of the moon and distant rising sun following behind. Artemis knew what would come wouldn't be easy, but she believed that with Jamie, they could work together to find a place in this world.

EPILOGUE

Life in the human world was still complicated. Noises were still too loud and unnatural. Lights were still far too bright. Other than the woods and the dangerous side roads, there was still too little nature to enjoy. Even the people weren't as open as her pack like Artemis had once hoped they would be. Yet, even with all this, both she and Jamie had found a peace that worked for them.

For Jamie, it was working with her dad to help other rescue centres gain protection for their animals and forests. Artemis loved watching them both work, especially Jamie.

The two would sit in the home's office talking back and forth, sometimes over top of the other in their discussion of how to move forward with permits and government requests. Jamie wore her glasses the most during those sessions, which, as Artemis watched her push them up the bridge of her nose as she studied the maps and figures in front of her, she couldn't help but think how cute she looked.

Jamie, of course, would catch her staring and offer her a sly wink before getting back to work.

Artemis would just smile and head out of the room to find something to entertain herself, which usually entailed her language lessons with a computer and a person she couldn't talk to or being cornered by Ritchie to watch movies with him when he was bored.

"You need a queer-ucation," he'd told her one day when he'd stopped by, a huge bag over his shoulder. "I have everything from sad to cheesy to classic. You must watch them all."

She had absolutely no idea what he was talking about, but she liked Ritchie, so she followed his lead.

When she wasn't invested in a new film recommended by Ritchie, having her lessons with Elder Will, or when Jamie was out working, Artemis would spend a lot of her time down at the Remembered Wood. Since its grand opening, Artemis had become its most frequent visitor.

The owner of the foundation, Elder Chase, had taken quite a shine to Artemis. When Artemis had arrived and Jamie had introduced the two of them, he had become instantly intrigued by Artemis's background. That interest quickly grew into a fast friendship with how often she visited and helped him out with the upkeep of the wood. He had lived on site since its opening, so Artemis always knew how to find him.

Elder Chase reminded her of Shadow, an elder with a secret passion that, no matter his age, pushed himself to do the most to help others. It was that familiarity that had Artemis returning so often to help him. She had the knowledge to do so as some of the plant life had grown within her family's territory. The last time she'd done it, she had warned Mr Chase about laying one of the memorial stones against one of the trees as "that one's roots grow upwards, it may hurt the memory".

He'd taken her suggestion right away and offered her a job immediately after.

She had no idea what a job was, but after a quick conversation on the phone that Jamie had given her, she accepted his offer. If it meant she could spend more time here, then this was perfect for her.

It had taken time, but after six months of living in the world with the humans, Artemis was finally starting to feel like herself.

"ARE YOU SURE YOU'RE READY FOR THIS?" JAMIE asked, a hand resting on Artemis's lower back. "There's no shame in sticking with—"

"I want to try." Artemis's grip tightened on the bars in front of her. "Mother always said that to be in balance with the world, we must fight with and against it. I have to take control and push ahead."

"Your mum sounds awesome," Jamie said with a smile. "Alright, I'll push you a little and then let go, OK?"

"OK."

"You have to keep your balance and peddle in rhythm, OK?"

Artemis turned and pressed a kiss to Jamie's cheek. "Yes."

Jamie's cheeks flushed a light, but she nodded and put a hand on top of Artemis's on the handlebars and lowered the other to the back of the seat. "Lift your feet up and get ready."

Putting her feet on the pedals of the bike Elder Will had given her, Artemis took a breath. She remembered being confused when he'd shown her the bike a few months ago, not knowing what it was until he'd explained. Elder Will had said he thought it may help her feel a little freer to be able to travel by herself when she needs to be alone. Artemis had been terrified of it for a period of time and, until this moment, had been using what Jamie had called stabilisers to ride the machine up and down the street.

"And we're off!" Jamie pushed the bike forward, and Artemis started to pedal. "You got this, I'm letting go now! Pedal!"

Her legs moved oddly and somewhat uncomfortably as Artemis pushed hard against the pedals. Her actions were awkward and her legs split open wide as she pushed and wobbled. Her balance wasn't right, but she was moving. She gripped the handlebars tighter and moved her legs fast as Jamie cheered from behind her. Artemis smiled in triumph.

Then she tipped sideways and fell.

"Ow…"

"Artemis!" Jamie cried, rushing to her side to pull her up from the hard ground. "Oh, my gosh." She unclipped the helmet Artemis had been wearing. "Are you okay, are you hu—"

With a tug, Artemis pulled Jamie towards her and locked their lips together. With Jamie's arms enveloped around her waist, she pulled her closer as she threw her own arms around Jamie's neck. She heard the bang of her helmet falling to the ground but paid it no mind.

"Get a room!" a young voice yelled from a distance, pulling the two women apart in surprise.

Across the road was a youngling cycling madly away in the opposite direction as if they were in danger. They looked at each other and burst out laughing.

Once they calmed down, Jamie tucked a piece of hair

behind Artemis's ear. "Not that I'm complaining, but what was all that for?"

Artemis took her hand. "It's a thank-you."

"For what?" Jamie asked, her voice as warm and deep as Artemis remembered it being when they were younglings.

"Because I…" Artemis began to smile. "I finally feel it."

"Feel what?"

Artemis lent her forehead against Jamie's.

"Home."

ACKNOWLEDGMENTS

While this is a combination of previously published shorts, I want to thank everyone again who helped bring these stories to life anyway.

To my lovely and supportive beta readers, Eli, Laurel Fredricks, Robert Gaymer, Michael Griswold, Emily Hu, K.C., Katie Mack, Isabel Pelech, Megs Peterson, Caitlin Santos, Andrea Septien, and Darien Smartt, thank you for bringing your honesty and help to making this series of shorts what they are now.

To Jeanie Y. Chang, thank you for helping me make sure that I was approaching Jamie and Seon-Mi (her mother) Korean culture and background sensitively.

To my phenomenal and consistently amazing editor, Carly Catt, you were and are a godsend and you helped make these stories as strong as they turned out to be.

And as always, a huge special thanks to my cover designer Ranpakoka for the brilliant art for these stories.

ABOUT THE AUTHOR

Francesca McMahon was born in Oxford, England, to a Scottish father and an Essex mother. They gained a B.A. in Creative Writing at Edge Hill University and was shortlisted for the university's Dame Janet Suzman Playwriting Award in 2019. Since graduating, Francesca went onto gain a Master's degree in the same subject and has continued to work on their writing of fantasy, horror, and romance fiction, as well as various tabletop RPGs and screenplays. As a queer person, their work is dedicated to the LGBTQIA+ community, and they hope that they will all find a home in their imaginary worlds.

You can learn more over at www.francescamcmahon.com or follow Francesca on social media, via Instagram, and TikTok (@adoseoffran).